Blame it on the MONSTERS

A tale of messy monster mayhem.

Written and Illustrated by

Richard A. Isbell

Blame it on the Monsters

ISBN-13:
978-1500727062

ISBN-10:
1500727067

This book is dedicated to my very patient family, whom I love deeply.

I would also like to thank the Veterans Writing Group, sponsored by the Writers Guild of America (East), for believing in a group of former military members. Because of you and the mentors you assigned to us, we are getting our stories and voices heard.

Why does our house look like it was hit by a train?
Well...it wasn't gangsters, mobsters or mutant lobsters.
Don't blame us, Mom, blame it on the

MONSTERS!

It started with a monster named Little White Lyle,
the sneakiest monster this side of the River Nile.
He knocked down all the cans in the grocery aisle!

Fluffy the five eyed flying floom made us do cart-wheels all around the living room. With automatic static fur, you're stuck to this monster and the room becomes a blur.

5

that smelled like a yak!

paddywack who raided my backpack looking for a snack.

one smack; my papers, my pencils and a gym socks

Everything is gone as he ate it in just

We didn't eat all the candy, no not one bite.
A silly Snack-O-Dile ate everything in sight.
She lives in the pantry, under the shelf.
Sneaking out at night to stuff herself.

How did everything get so wet?

When it comes to water it's a sure bet

that a rub-a-dub scrub named Grub

was practicing cannonballs in the tub!

And that piece of missing cake?
That had to be Jake the Psychedelic Snake!

There's a stalk eyed Looky-Loo named Mr. Spark,

His eyes really glow and he can see in the dark!

No hiding place is safe with this guy around.

He told us what our presents were and where they can be found.

14

The remote isn't working for the TV you say?
We saw a one-eyed monster in your chair yesterday.
She clicked through the channels as quick as you please.
We're thinking she dropped it in a bowl of nacho cheese!

Why am I still awake?
Well it's the monsters under my bed for goodness sake!
They're playing football, jacks and air guitar with a rake.

Bouncing on the bed was a Googly-Eyed Gallump

He launched me in the air with one big jump!

A monster named Paul
painted those pictures on the wall.
It couldn't have been us,
because we're just not that tall!

Why is our kitchen covered in jelly? We tried to stop a grape monster named Big Mary Shelly. Our hands got all sticky and smelly as they sank into her great big belly.

21

Start Why are we bouncing off the walls?

We may have had too much soda, cookies

and malted milk balls. A giant

Monster gave us candy and other

assorted treats to see how

far up the wall we could go

without cleats and

other amazing feats!

24

Stop this right now, we heard our mother cry
This is all nonsense and it's just one big lie!
Blaming the monsters is as silly as it sounded
I don't want to hear anymore, you're all grounded!

Good bye, Lenny
Good bye, Jake
Good bye, Snack-o-dile
and the Psychedelic Snake.

Because a lie is a lie
and no matter what you figure,
It grows like these monsters
and gets bigger and bigger,

28

Biography of Richard A. Isbell,
Artist & Writer

Richard Isbell started his love for art, cartoons and comics at an early age. After showing his mother that he could draw the cartoons from the funny papers at age 5, his parents went out and bought him his first sketch book and have been supportive ever since.

He grew up in a little town with one stop light named Bellbrook, Ohio. Richard joined the Air Force straight out of high school and was lucky enough to be stationed in many places in the US and Europe. After serving in support of Operation Desert Shield/Desert Storm he returned home to rehabilitate by attending the Columbus College of Art and Design where he graduated with a B.A. in Fine Arts and Illustration.

Richard is a published illustrator, graphic designer and cartoonist. He has produced book covers, made cartoons for newspapers, designed logos, created theatre posters and painted murals all over the world. He lives in Columbus, Ohio with his wife Yvonne, his kids Devyn, Ricky and Ravyn and their four cats.

Made in the USA
Lexington, KY
25 November 2016